TEN TERRIFIC TALES

... and two bonus stories

Frederick Bethke

ISBN-13 979-8346191568

Cover design by Freepik

The author thanks the members of the Petaluma Village Network for their encouragement and support.

Special thanks to Stella Allison and Jennifer Bethke for editing and formatting assistance.

CONTENTS

... AND TWO BONUS STORIES

RHONDA RIDES THE RANGE

Rhonda liked to ride the range. Horses were fine, but she preferred other steeds.

Rhonda liked to ride on a bison. "This shaggy fur is easy to hold onto. Yahoo!" said Rhonda.

Rhonda liked to ride on an elk. "These antlers make great handlebars. Yahoo!" cried Rhonda.

Rhonda liked to ride on a Rocky Mountain sheep. "If these horns would work, I could go Oogah! Oogah! Yahoo!" laughed Rhonda.

Rhonda liked to ride on pronghorn antelopes. Since they were slender, she used a pair – one for each foot. "Double yahoo!" yelled Rhonda.

One day, Rhonda was sitting in her kitchen. She looked at the stove. "Hmm," thought Rhonda. "A stove is also called a range." Rhonda dragged the stove out into the yard. She got some rope, and climbed aboard.

"Yahoo! I'm riding the range!

Yahoo!" yelled Rhonda.

"Call the doctors!" yelled the neighbors.

The doctors came. Rhonda was deranged.

DOWN AT THE STATION

"Just calm down. It's OK. You're safe here. Calm down. Take some deep breaths. There. Feeling better?"

"Yes, thank you."

"Good. Now just start at the beginning and tell me what happened."

"Well, I work at the furniture

factory over there on Pine Street. I'm in the tuffet department. Each morning at ten, we have our break. If the weather's nice, I like to take a tuffet and go into that big open field behind the building, and sit on the tuffet in the sunshine and have a little snack. Some people like a donut, some like an orange or an apple, but I like curds and whey."

"Kurzenway? What is that – some kind of energy bar?"

"No, curds and whey. But that's not important. Well, while I was seated there on my tuffet, enjoying the sunshine and my snack, suddenly a shadow covered me. I looked up, and a huge, horrible black hairy spider had sat down beside me!

"It's a wonder I didn't die of fright right on the spot. I screamed and ran away as fast as I could, and ran right over here to the police station. Officer, you've got to do something. That horrible giant spider is a menace!"

"I see. Did this spider hurt you?"

"He scared the life out of me."

"But did he touch you?"

"I didn't give him the chance – I ran away so quick."

"Did he threaten you?"

"I don't think spiders can talk."

"Larry, is that right? Can spiders talk?"

"Uh ... I don't think so, Sarge."

"So, he didn't harm you or touch you or threaten you. And that's public land back there, so he wasn't trespassing. I don't think we can actually charge him with a crime."

"But there has to be a law against scaring people half to death."

"I'm sorry he upset you. Here's what I'll do ... what was your name again?"

"Muffet."

"So, Mrs. Muffet ..."

"That's Miss Muffet."

"So Miss Muffet, when the captain comes in this afternoon, I'll talk to him. If there's anything that can be done, he'll give you a call."

"Oh, no!"

"What's wrong?"

"I just realized I left the tuffet out there in the meadow. And my spoon and bowl, too. And that horrible monster is probably still there, waiting to pounce."

"Not to worry, Officer Larry here will drive you over there. You can stay safe in the squad car with the doors locked and the windows rolled up, and Officer Larry will retrieve your belongings. And don't worry about Larry's weight problem. He's actually fairly competent."

"I'll talk to you later, Sarge. OK Miss Muffet, let's go."

"But surely you're not going like that, are you? Where are your guns? You are going to need four or five guns, at least. And a ... a ... a fire tosser."

"Fire tosser? Oh, you mean a flame thrower?"

"Yes, a flame thrower. You officers don't seem to understand. This is a monster of a spider, black and hairy and evil. He's huge. He has lots of beady eyes. And he's taller than I am. Officer Sergeant, you may never see Officer Larry again. And then you'll be sorry."

"Hmm ... Maybe yes, maybe no."

"I'll talk to you later, Sarge. OK, Miss Muffet, let's go."

"Oh, Miss Muffet. One more question. That Kurzenway stuff you were drinking ..."

"It's curds and whey. Curds. And. Whey. And you don't drink it. You eat it."

"Either way, is it fermented?"

"Fermented? No. Curds and whey is not fermented. It's .... Oh, I see what you're getting at. And I resent that insinuation. I am not inebriated. I do not drink alcohol ... in the morning. Huh! Fermented curds and whey. The very idea. Come, Officer Larry, we are leaving."

THAT CHERRY TREE

"George, come here! Look at my cherry tree!"

"Wow, Dad. Looks like a beaver got it."

"No, George."

"Or a woodchuck."

"No."

"Or a very strong wind."

"George, I know hatchet marks when I see them. And whose father very foolishly gave his son a little hatchet for his birthday just last week?"

"Pure coincidence, Dad."

"You deny chopping down the cherry tree?"

"Absolutely."

"George, where were you this morning?"

"Down at the church with the bible study group."

"George, that group meets on Thursdays. This is Tuesday."

"I misspoke, Dad. I meant to say I was in my room studying the bible."

"Would that be the bible your Aunt Clara sent you last year?"

"That very one."

"George, I happen to know that book is still in its original package. It's never been opened. George, do you still deny you did this?"

"Dad, don't you remember the Boy's Code of Conduct? Always

deny everything? You were a boy once yourself, Dad."

"George, I think the evidence is clear. I find you guilty, and there must be a punishment. So I say, no dessert for you tonight."

"Aw, Dad."

"And guess what we're having."

"Oh no!"

"Oh yes. Your favorite – cherry pie."

"How about half a slice?"

"No."

"Just the tip of the triangle?"

"No George. So now you see the results of your misbehavior."

"Speaking of seeing, Dad, when I walk down the hall, I go past the library."

"So?"

"If that library door isn't closed all the way, I see what's going on in there."

"What are you saying, George?"

"Dad, do you know Sarah?"

"Absolutely not."

"Sarah the maid?"

"I deny everything."

"Dad, I've heard that when a fellow is starving to death, like from lack of dessert, he can become very talkative."

"What are you suggesting, George?"

"A quid pro quo, Dad."

"I see your Latin tutor has been doing a good job. Well, it seems I have little choice. So I hereby revoke the no-dessert order. You can have your pie, George."

"Gee, thanks Dad. An extra large slice would be appreciated."

"I'll see what I can do.

"You know, George, all this discussing and denying and revoking has made me a little hungry. What do you say we try to sneak into the kitchen and get some pie before dinner."

"Great idea, Dad. Follow me – I know the best way."

"You've done this before, George?"

"Many times, Dad."

"George, my boy, your future is bright."

AT THE CROSSROADS

Coming towards the crossroads from the west were the United Porcupines of Polk County. They were on their way to a conference, where they expected lots of arguing. They were already feeling annoyed.

Coming down from the north was the Associated Acupuncturists Darts Team. Each member carried three sets – a practice set, heavies for windy conditions, and a decorated set for tournaments. They practiced as they walked along, flicking their darts into signs and posts and trees.

Coming up from the south was an ancient van. On one side it said *Pierre LaPointe: Purveyor of Fine Tacks, Needles, and Pins*. And below in smaller letters: *Needles for haystacks our specialty*. On the other side, a sign urged the public to *Come to the point*. Pierre's rattletrap van had occasional brakes and suspect steering.

And coming from the east was Balthazar the Balloon Man. Tied on his wagon were hundreds, thousands of balloons, of all shapes and colors. He had worked all morning inflating them. Among them were a great many animal balloons. Especially dogs. Balthazar loved making dog balloons.

As cruel fate would have it, all four parties arrived at the crossroads simultaneously.

Seeing their ancient enemy, the dog, the porcupines rushed furiously forward. The darts team praised their good fortune, and let fly. Pierre stomped on his nonexistent brakes and yanked the wheel to the side, but the van rolled over, spewing forth a glittering steel cloud of tacks, needles, and pins.

The carnage was considerable.

After the others had left, Balthazar was alone, sitting on a stone by the side of the road. As he plucked quills and darts and needles from his clothing, he reminisced. "This reminds me of another incident at another crossroads. That time, I ran into the Society of Spiny Echidnas, the Amphibious Sticklebacks Walking Club, and the Tri-State Triceratops Impersonators. It rained rubber fragments for an hour."

Balthazar sighed, and was silent for quite some time. "Maybe I can cheer myself up if I make a balloon dog," he said.

And he did.

BEAMING UP AND DOWN

"So Albert, have you read the disclosure? What do you say?"

"Yes, Mr. XL3, and ..."

"Oh, just a second, I skipped something. Let's see here ... one, two, three, four. That's right, isn't it?"

"Is what right?"

"Number of limbs for your species?"

"Uh, two arms, two legs – Yes, four."

"Because sometimes mistakes are made in the upbeaming. See that fellow over there with the green badge? That's ZB9. He runs the upbeam machine. His green badge means rookie. He's fresh out of school, and this is his first voyage. He's already made quite a few mistakes, some of them rather amusing, I must admit.

"But back to business. Are you ready to sign the release form?"

"Well, Mr. XL3, I'm grateful to you for giving me this ride."

"Yes, we saw you down there struggling along with that odd stick under your arm."

"A crutch, we call it."

"Crutch, yes, crutch. And we thought we'd help and give you a ride. So! What do you say?"

"Well, I don't want to seem ungrateful and all that, but I think I'll decline your offer."

"What? Decline? Really? I'm surprised at you, Albert. Aren't you interested in science?"

"Well sure, but ..."

"Don't you want to advance knowledge?"

"I'm all for that, but ... I mean ... dissection! That's pretty serious."

"Of course it's serious. Science is a serious business. I must say, I'm disappointed in you, Albert. You looked like someone eager for learning."

"Please, Mr. XL3, I don't want to be ungrateful, but could you just put me back down where you found me?"

"All right, Albert. But before you go, take a look at these four-color glossy brochures. In addition to our scientific work, we offer tours of the galaxy. Reasonably priced. Here, this one is my favorite. We fly you right through the heart of a black hole. And, as a courtesy to our travelers, we fill out your postcards for you. Because, to tell the truth, you're a bit incoherent for a while after that unique experience."

"That's nice, but right now I'd just like to get back down."

"Down it is, then. All set over there, ZB9? Goodbye, Albert.

"No no no, ZB9, you idiot! Not on top of the palm tree. Put him on the sidewalk. Aim for the center of the sidewalk. OK, now try it again. Steady ...

"Oh my stars! You bungler, ZB9. Now look what you've done. Sorry down there! Sorry, Albert! Sorry! Yes, yes I know. A picket fence does hurt a lot. We apologize.

"ZB9! You moron, when we get back to base, you're going straight into remedial training. Now the poor guy needs two crutches."

BREMENSTADT MUSICIANS, ACT II

In their little house in the forest, the animals were relaxing. The donkey was in the rocking chair reading the newspaper. The rooster was pecking at some kernels in his dish. The cat was snoozing on the rug. And the dog was standing by the window, looking out into the trees.

"You know," the dog said, "we

call ourselves the Bremenstadt Musicians, but we never got to Bremen. We've never been to Bremen. We should go some day."

Great idea! And just like that, off they set, down the road through the forest.

After a few hours, the dog said, "Did anybody bring snacks?"

"Not I," said the donkey.

"Not I," said the rooster.

"Not I," said the cat.

The road crossed a large meadow. The sun was beating down. There was no shade. "Did anybody bring our hats?" asked the donkey.

"Not I," said the dog.

"Not I," said the rooster

"Not I," said the cat.

The road reentered the forest. It seemed to go on forever. "How far is it to Bremen?" asked the rooster. No one knew. "Did anyone bring a map?"

"Not I," said the donkey.

"Not I," said the dog.

"Not I," said the cat.

Then the road came to a river. A wide river. There was no bridge.

"Hmm," said the dog.

"Hmm," said the rooster.

"Hmm," said the cat.

"I know!" said the donkey. "We can make our famous tower, and then I can wade us across."

Great idea! So the dog climbed up on the donkey's back, the cat climbed up on the dog's back, and the rooster got up on the cat's back. Slowly and carefully, the donkey waded out into the river. All went well at first, but then his feet left the bottom, and he was swimming.

"I have a terrible itch behind my left ear," said the dog.

"Don't scratch it!" cried the

others. But the dog lifted his hind leg, and down crashed the tower. Resurfacing, they struggled back to the bank and crawled out, panting and dripping.

"Whew!" Said the dog. "I'm glad we could all do the dog paddle."

"Not I," said the cat. "The cat paddle is what saved me."

A general retreat was agreed upon. It was past midnight when they finally reached the little house in the forest, and they quickly fell asleep.

The next morning, the donkey was in the rocking chair reading the newspaper, the rooster was pecking at some kernels in his dish, the cat was snoozing on the rug, and the dog was standing by the window, looking out into the trees. "It's a shame we didn't get to Bremen," he said. The others were silent. After some time, the dog said "Maybe we should try again someday."

"Maybe," said the others. "Some day."

FIRST IN LINE

Clerk: "How do you like this color? A nice cheerful green."

He: "Yeah, I like it."

She: "Oh, I don't know. It's awfully bright."

Clerk: "We have lots of other shades. Here's a medium green, and this one is a grayish green. Almost any shade you want.

"We also have them in different shapes. Here's a model that accents the lobes. Here's one that's almost round. And this model is quite attractive. The edges curl."

She: "Ooh! I like that one. But is there just one size?"

He: "Yeah, is this a one-size-fits-all deal?"

Clerk: "Not at all, sir. We have a wide range of sizes – from XM to AR."

He: "XM? Extra Medium?"

Clerk: "Extra Modest. And AR is Almost Risqué."

She: "But they're all this one-piece design?"

Clerk: "I understand Madame's concern. If you'll just step over to this other counter, you'll find two-piece and three-piece models. Here is a nice two-piece."

She: "Oh, I don't think so. It's so big. It looks like a bib."

Clerk: "Well then, we have the three-piece."

She: "How do you ... put those on?"

Clerk: "Simply turn it over, apply a dab of tree sap to the underside, and then affix it to

Madame's ... (ahem) you know. Why not try it on. Yes, that's right. Now step over to the mirror."

She: "Adam, what do you think?"

He: "Frankly, my dear, I prefer you in the one-piece."

She: "Well, let's go back to the first counter then."

He: "What is this material, exactly?"

Clerk: "That, sir, is genuine fig leaf. Comfortable, but sturdy and long-lasting."

He: "Won't chafe?"

Clerk: "Oh no.

"So ... have you folks made a decision?"

He: "Yes. We're going to go with the gray-green color, this medium size, and the one-piece for us both."

Clerk: "Excellent choices. The gray-green shows humility and that size is a good compromise between modesty and suggestiveness. And, if I may say so, the au naturel approach up top shows Madame to best advantage."

She: "Oh, I bet you say that to all the fallen women."

Clerk: "Actually, you're the first. But I hear that there will be quite a line in years to come.

"Now, since you are our first customers, there's no charge. And you have a lifetime guarantee. If your fig leaves show signs of wear or begin to wither, simply come back to the shop and we'll replace them gratis."

He: "Gee, thanks. You're an angel. You know, I really like those wings you're wearing. Do you sell those here, too?"

Clerk: "I'm sorry, sir, this is clothing only."

He: "Well, how can I get a pair?"

Clerk: "That's a rather complicated subject, sir. Better left for another discussion.

"Now, shall I wrap them up, or will you be wearing them immediately?"

He: "I think the commandment was to put them on right away."

Clerk: "Very good. Well, I wish you both the best of luck out there in the wide world. Stay away from serpents. And watch out for high winds. Goodbye, goodbye."

THE TALE OF MISTER INKY

Mister Inky kept close to the buildings when he walked downtown, one shoulder brushing the bricks, putting maximum distance between himself and the street. For Mister Inky lived in Steamrollerville.

The massive machines were everywhere. Some were orange. Some were yellow. Some were black. But all were large and dangerous. They clanked through the streets, crunching up over the curbs, knocking over the lampposts, flattening the parking meters.

Intersections were particularly perilous. Steamrollers came at you from all directions – from the left, from the right, from straight ahead, and – worst of all – rolling up on you from behind. So Mister Inky was always very cautious.

Mondays through Fridays, Mister Inky worked for a printing company. On Saturdays, he worked a second job in a school supply warehouse. He worked this second job to save up money. Money for a ticket. A ticket to anywhere. Anywhere out of Steamrollerville.

One fine spring day, Mister Inky was out for a walk. He sported a handsome new hat, a dapper affair of cream-colored straw, with a festive band of green and gold silk. A very unusual purchase for Mister Inky, but he had been intoxicated by the delicious spring weather.

But then as he walked along, the mischievous wind snatched the hat from Mister Inky's head and sent it spinning across the road. Mister Inky gave chase.

Poor Mister Inky.

He became instantly two-dimensional. Totally horizontal. Absolutely without verticality. Poor Mister Inky.

So, was that the end of Mister Inky?

Someday, you might be in a special doctor's office, and you might be shown some pictures. "Hey!" you will exclaim. "It's Mister Inky!" The doctor will frown. But you will know better.

It is Mister Inky. Mister Inky, the Immortal.

THE DOUBLE SINGLE

"We're fortunate to have with us today a player from the early days of baseball – Mr. Lucky Logan. Welcome, Lucky."

"That's not my real name, you know. It's Aloysius. Aloysius Oglethorpe Logan. But you can call me Lucky."

"Great."

"How do you like my new sport coat?"

"Very ... striking. I don't think I've ever seen that combination of stripes and plaid before."

"Pretty snazzy, huh? I always was a snappy dresser."

“Lucky, let's talk baseball. I think the fans would like to hear about the time you hit the double single."

"Right, the double single. Well, it was in one of the first games of the season. We opened against the Birdsville Buzzards. We expected to face Blazer Zipowtz, the fastball king. But when we looked out of the dugout, it wasn’t Blazer on the mound."

"Not Blazer?"

"No. Blazer's a big tall fellah. This was a little guy. So we figured they'd traded off-season and got Shorty McGrew. Shorty wasn't very big, but he was a mighty fine pitcher.

"Then the game starts, and we're slamming the old horsehide all over the lot. Everybody's tearing the cover off the ball – doubles, triples, homers. We figure Shorty hurt his arm in the off-season rolling beer barrels or something. We win that game 87-3.

"And the second game is more of the same. The scoreboard guy is getting worried, cuz there's only two slots for numbers. Finally he has to get a ladder and nail a number one in front, cuz we win that game 104-2."

"Amazing."

"Yeah. But then a nosey reporter poked around in the locker room, and found out that's not Shorty McGrew on the mound. Blazer's still on the roster, but he's stuck on the West Coast, cuz of a train strike. Their manager was short of players, so that's their batboy pitching."

"Their batboy?"

"Well, the poor kid. The uniform was flopping around on him, cap falling over his eyes, shoes four sizes too big. He was trying as hard as he could, but his fastball just floated up to the plate like a marshmallow, and his change-up didn't change, and his curveball didn't curve, and his slider didn't slide. So we were murdering the ball, having a picnic up there at the plate."

"But Lucky, what about the double single?"

"Right, the double single. Well, in one of those games, I was at the plate, and the little batboy tried so hard on a pitch that on his follow-through one of his shoes came off. So the ball is coming towards the plate and the shoe is coming towards the plate.

"Well, the ball arrives first, and I hammer that baby into left field. Then the shoe arrives, and I whack it over the second baseman's head. I chug down the line, the right fielder retrieves the shoe and pegs it to first, but I beat the shoe, so I'm safe on first with a single. And the ball I hit to left took one big hop and went over the fence for a ground-rule double."

"So you had a double and a single."

"Yeah! Well, the umps are

staring at each other with their mouths open. They don't know what to do. They call a big conference and talk forever.

"The fans are drifting off to the beer stands. Finally the umps see it this way. Two, plus one, equals three. A double plus a single makes a triple. So they put me on third."

"So you're on third with a triple."

"Yeah. But not for long. I got picked off on the very next play. That batboy was a tricky little devil.

"But in the third game, our luck ran out. Blazer was back on the mound. Seems he, uh, sort of borrowed a car and drove non-stop across the country to rejoin his team. But he still had enough moxie to pitch a shutout. We only got two hits. I struck out four times. But I did get a couple of foul tips. That was pretty good against Blazer."

"And the rest of the season?"

"Well, we lost most of our games, and ended up in the cellar. As usual."

"Fascinating. But now I'd like to switch gears and talk about the defensive aspects of the game."

"Oh let's not."

"Most fans know about the Gold Glove award, given to the best fielder. What they might not know is that in the very early days, there was another award, given to the worst fielder. That was the Mister Muffer award."

"Never heard of it."

"Lucky, it says here you won that award."

"Must be a misprint."

"Lucky, it says you won that award five seasons in a row."

"That book is full of errors. Can't be trusted."

"Lucky, our listeners may be wondering. With that kind of fielding, and your lifetime batting average of 178 ..."

"178, 378, something like that."

"... How was it that you managed to stay in the big league for so many years?"

"Well, I suppose I can talk about it now. It was so many years ago. You see, there was this girl."

"A girl?"

"Yeah. Trixie."

"Trixie?"

"Trixie. She worked in the souvenir shop at the ballpark. Well, one day, by accident, a piece of information just fell into my lap."

"Concerning Trixie?"

"Concerning Trixie, and the owner of the ball club."

"Ah!"

"Yeah. So he and I had a little conversation. And, as a result of which, I got this really nice multi-year no-cut contract. So I stayed with the club for many seasons."

"Well, I see we're about out of time. Thank you for being with us today, Mister Lucky Logan."

"You're welcome. Would you like to hear about when I hid the shortstop's underwear?"

"Perhaps another day, Lucky. We're out of time."

"You see, he was –

[Cut to black and silence.]

THE GOLDILOCKS TEST LAB

It took Goldilocks quite some time to calm down after the incident with the Three Bears. But when she finally did, she grew restless. "I need something to do," she told herself. "What can I do? What am I good at?"

She tried the piano, but her right hand and left hand would never coordinate. She tried embroidery, but that turned into unintentional acupuncture. She tried painting, but her still lifes turned into abstracts, and her abstracts into mud.

"Isn't there anything I'm good at?" cried Goldilocks. "There must be something I can do." Then it struck her. "Yes! I'm very discriminating. I have excellent taste."

So Goldilocks opened a test lab. She tested tools, and fabrics, and lotions, and kitchen utensils – anything and everything. "Hmm," she would say. "That ladle handle is too thick. And that one is too slender. But this handle, this handle is just right."

Of course, furniture and food were her specialties. "Hmm. The armrests on that chair are too high. And those are a bit low. But these, these are just right." And, “That soup has too much salt and pepper, and that other sample is bland, but this soup, this one is just right.”

The lab was a success. Companies valued her judgment. Business boomed. I could use some help, thought Goldilocks.

She tried Hansel and Gretel, but if it wasn't candy, they lost interest. She sent for Jack and Jill, but on the way to the lab, they stopped for a drink, and suffered serious injury. She had high hopes for Mr. and Mrs. Jack Sprat. But they would come to her and say “Look! We've licked the platters clean again!" "Very nice," said Goldilocks, "but not exactly what we're after."

So she did all the testing herself. It meant long hours and lots of work. But she liked being busy.

Then, late one night as she was finishing up the day's paperwork, she sighed. "Something is wrong. The Just Right lab is a success, I'm getting rich, I’m famous, but ..." She put down her pencil and stared out the window into the night. Then it dawned on her. "Aha! Yes, that's what's wrong!"

So Goldilocks sat down and wrote a very sincere letter of apology to the Three Bears. She sent it to them express, along with a crate of gourmet porridge, a hundred pounds of filet mignon, a barrel of honey, brand new sets of the finest living room and bedroom furniture, and a bouquet of flowers.

The Bears forgave her. "Ahh," said Goldilocks. "Now I feel better. That was the just right thing to do."

BONUS STORY: JABBERWOCK JUNIOR

The Widow Jabberwock was talking to her son. "Be very careful out there. Watch what you're doing. Use your head. Stay away from the Tulgey Wood. Remember what happened to your father! Don't go around annoying humans. Especially humans with swords. Most especially humans with vorpal swords. And don't hang around with that Bandersnatch kid. He's a bad influence. That whole Bandersnatch clan is nothing but trouble."

But Junior Jabberwock heard none of this. Good advice did not even go in one ear and out the other. Good advice simply bounced off his skull, like ping-pong balls off a Galapagos tortoise.

"Oh, I don't know why I bother," sighed poor Mrs. Jabberwock.

Off dashed Junior, and ran straight to the house of the Bandersnatch kid. "Come on," he called. "Let's go." Off they went on their ramble. The Jubjub bird was singing in the Tumtum tree, but paused to watch them pass underneath, cocking its head in curiosity.

Straight to the Tulgey Wood they went. There, they saw a human. The human had no vorpal sword. He had no sword of any kind. Not even a jackknife. Not even a pointy stick. Junior gobbled him down.

"Hey!" objected the Bandersnatch kid frumiously. "You didn't share!"

"Of course not," replied Junior. "I'm a Jabberwock."

BONUS STORY: GRAND OPENING

BB1: "I can't believe it. I can't believe he did that."

BB2: "Take it easy."

BB1: "All our hard work – ruined. Where is he? I'll strangle him. That birdbrain!"

BB2: "Hey, watch your language."

BB1: "Oops. Sorry. That moron,

that cretin. How could he do such a thing?"

BB2: "Maybe it was oxygen deprivation."

BB1: "Oxygen what?"

BB2: "We were all crammed into that tight space – all twenty-four of us. Not much air. We were only supposed to be in there while they carried us to the table. But something went wrong. I could hear the waiters yelling at each other. We were in there a long time. I was getting light-headed myself."

BB1: "That's no excuse. Two months of rehearsing. You know

how hard Bach is – four-part harmony, all that counterpoint. All down the drain because of that idiot. Our big moment. Our royal debut. We're set before the king, the pie is opened, I'm just giving the down beat, and that moron yells Cock-a-Doodle-Doo! What a disaster."

BB2: "Well, it got a big laugh."

BB1: "Sure. And everyone was laughing so loud, nobody could hear our singing."

BB2: "You know, maybe we should try switching to comedy."

BB1: "What? Cheap jokes? Never. Bach and Mozart and

Haydn would roll in their graves. Oh oh! Here comes the king's councilor. Now we're in trouble."

BB2: "I don't think so. He's smiling."

KC: "Well, well, well. That was very amusing. The king is still chuckling. He's asked me to award each one of you a sixpence. And he's had the servants set out big sacks of rye seed in the courtyard. You can fill your pockets as you leave."

BB2: "We don't have pockets."

KC: "Well, take it any way you want. We're all glad you cheered the king up. He's been grumpy –

ever since the queen started avoiding him, locking herself in the parlor and stuffing herself with bread and honey. And then when he goes into his counting house and counts out his money, he gets a different total each time, and that makes him even more irritable. Believe me, there's nothing more dangerous than a grouchy king. So all of us courtiers thank you.

"However, there is some bad news. When one of the maids was in the garden hanging out the clothes, she suffered a grievous injury. And it seems the culprit was a blackbird."

BB1: "But it couldn't have been

any of us. We've all been inside since we arrived."

KC: "It doesn't matter. That maid was the king's favorite, and when he finds out, the fur is going to fly. Or in your case, the feathers. So I suggest you leave quickly."

BB1: "But we were hoping for a position as Royal Choristers."

KC: "Out of the question."

BB2: "How about as Royal Comedians?"

KC: "We don't need twenty-four court jesters. But here's a tip. Ten miles down the road, just after you cross the border, you'll see a large castle. That belongs to Old King Cole. I understand he's getting awfully tired of fiddle music. You could try for a job there. Well, thanks again, and good luck."

BB1: "Guess we'd better round up the boys and take wing."

BB2: "Yeah. You know, as we fly along, we could work on some comedy routines. Knock knock."

BB1: "Cut it out, or I'll knock knock you on the head."

BB2: "Hey! That could work. I say knock knock, and then you say OK, knock knock, and you bop me on the head twice with a foam rubber mallet. Hilarious, right?"

BB1: "Oh for gosh sakes. Forgive them Johann Sebastian, for they know not what they do. Let's go."

Made in the USA
Middletown, DE
07 February 2025